W9-CZN-098

Night Walk to the Sea

A Story About Rachel Carson, Earth's Protector

By DEBORAH WILES   *Pictures by* DANIEL MIYARES

schwartz & wade books · new york

*I*t was bedtime in Rachel's cabin
in the woods,
when thunder BOOMED and
the storm roared in.

"I'm not afraid!" shouted Roger.
CRAAAAACK! the thunder answered.

Roger's heart thumped in his chest.

"I don't want to go to bed!" he shouted.

He stomped across the floor in his Godzilla pajamas.

"I am a monster!"

"You *are*, sometimes," Rachel agreed.

She laughed and pretended to be a monster with Roger.

Then—

FITZZZZZ!—

the lights went out.

She lighted a lantern, then

wrapped Roger's small body
in the big blanket
and sat with him in the window seat
so they could watch the storm together.

But Roger wriggled and twisted in Rachel's arms.
"I want the lights on!" he shouted.

When the storm had worn itself out, Rachel said,
"Let's go for a night walk to the sea.
We haven't done that in a long time."

Rachel helped Roger with his rain jacket and boots.

The boots were green, with fangs on them.

"Grrrrrr!" said Roger. "I'm not afraid!"

"That's good," said Rachel,

"because there is nothing to be afraid of.

The whole world is waiting for you."

They walked past the cinnamon ferns
and reindeer moss
and the *drip-drip-drip* of glittery raindrops
on the tips of the shiny leaves
that were washed in moonlight.
Their flashlights bobbed cones of yellow light ahead of them.

"Listen to the voices of living things," said Rachel.
A screech owl softly called to its mate
from an old woodpecker hole:
tremelo-tremelo-thrum-thrum-thrum.

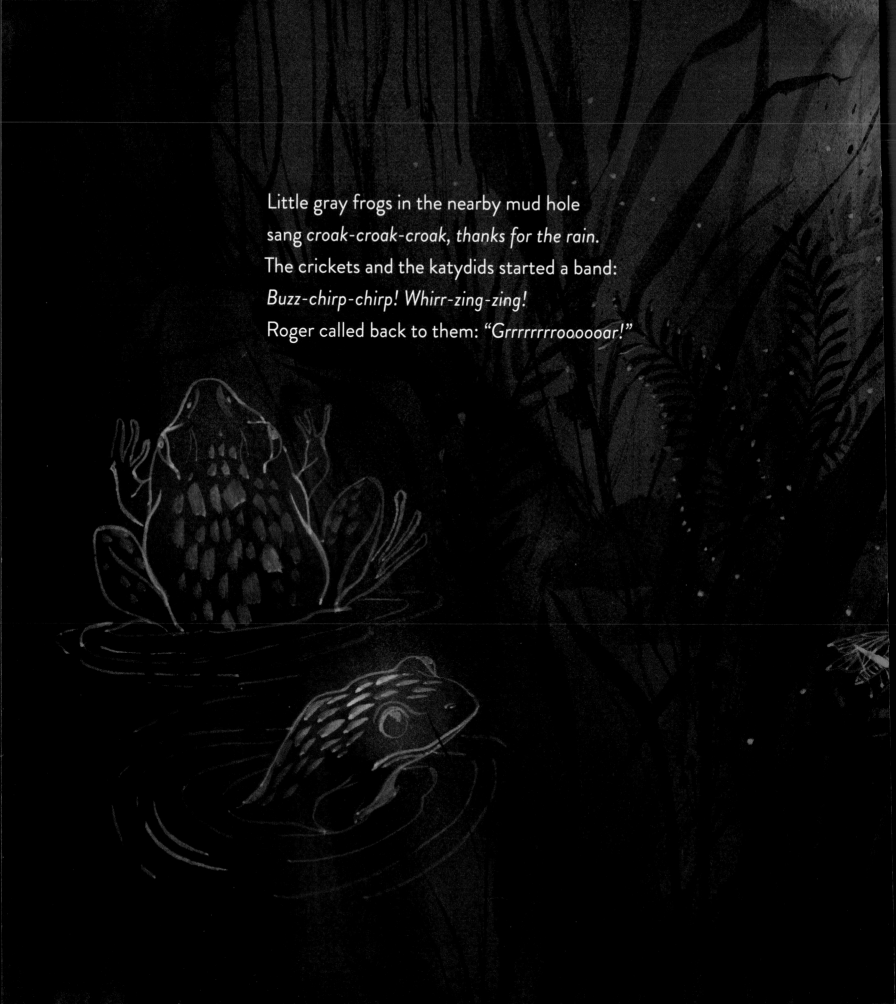

Little gray frogs in the nearby mud hole
sang *croak-croak-croak, thanks for the rain.*
The crickets and the katydids started a band:
Buzz-chirp-chirp! Whirr-zing-zing!
Roger called back to them: "*Grrrrrrrrrooooooar!*"

Down the wooden stairs,
past the laurel and the blueberry bushes,
they stepped until they reached the salty shore.

The roosting shorebirds flushed up and *away-away-away.*
Roger tromped across the beach,
crunch-crunch-crunch!

He stomped the waves that
bubbled and burbled around his monstery boots.
"I will crush you!" he shouted
while the ghost crabs tunneled
ahead of his boots
into the wet sand.
Roger's heart banged in his chest,
harder and faster,
until he was all stomped out.

"Come here," said Rachel in her softest voice.

Roger came.

"Turn off your flashlight."

Roger did.

"Close your eyes."

Roger closed them.

And then, as the soft dark folded itself around them,

and the sea called to them, in and out, in and out,

like a lullaby,

Roger and Rachel breathed in the salty sea air . . .

together.

"Now open your eyes," said Rachel. "Look!"
Roger blinked. "What is it?" he whispered.

The sea was *alive* with moving light.
Blue and green and sparkling like diamonds,
glittering like emeralds,
alive and alive and alive.

the sea was filled with luminous life.

"They are thousands of tiny organisms that live in the sea,"
Rachel explained, "like little will-o'-the-wisps.
The storm must have stirred them up,
and they've turned on their lights."

"Look at this one!" said Roger.
A tiny creature was at their feet,
blinking furiously in the foam,
wet and frantic.
"He's trying to get to the lights in the sea!"

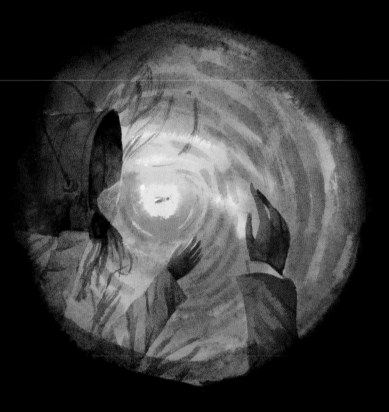

"It's a firefly," said Rachel.
"He doesn't belong in the sea.
He must have lost his way in the storm."

"Will he die?" asked Roger.
"Not if we save him," said Rachel.
"Quick! Use your bucket."

Roger scooped up the firefly along with
sand and seaweed and salt water.
"Here," said Rachel, "let's put him in my bucket so he can dry out."

As carefully as the most gentle monster,
Roger helped Rachel take the drowning firefly
out of his waterlogged bucket and
put it into her dry one.
"I'll carry it," he announced. And he did.

They left the sea and
picked their way past the juniper and thistles,
climbed over the rocks, up the steps, and
to the cabin in the woods.

Roger's heart thrummed gently in his chest while
he watched the firefly signal with its light,
stronger and brighter,
like a tiny firefly roar.

"He is so little," said Roger.
"And you are so big," said Rachel.
"I want to send him home," said Roger.
And that is what they did.

They released the firefly, who was dry enough to fly again.
They watched it flit and circle and wink away
into the woods that were waiting for it.

Roger rubbed his eyes.

"I am a monster who saves fireflies."

"You are indeed," said Rachel.

"And you are also a boy who loves
all the creatures of the woods and sea.
You are their brave protector."

"Sometimes I forget," whispered Roger.
Rachel tucked Roger into bed.
"I will help you remember."

"I think that firefly was afraid," Roger said, sleepy now.

"All of us are afraid sometimes," answered Rachel.

"*Grrrrrr . . . ,*" Roger whispered,
which made them both laugh.

And as the lights danced outside Roger's window,
Rachel kissed him goodnight.

A Note About Rachel Carson
and This Story

I sincerely believe . . . it is not half so important to *know* as to *feel*. —Rachel Carson, *The Sense of Wonder*

Rachel Louise Carson (1907–1964) grew up in Springdale, Pennsylvania, far from the sea. As a child she rambled, often with her mother, who encouraged her quiet wondering and wandering through the woods and fields near her home. She felt drawn to the nearby Allegheny River—where did it lead? When she found a fossil shell while digging nearby, she wondered about the ocean creatures that had once lived there. What were they like?

Rachel became a writer, an ecologist, and a marine scientist who wrote with great passion and respect about the natural world. She is the celebrated author of *Silent Spring*, one of the first books to document the deadly effects of widespread chemical pesticides on the earth and all living things.

But her first love was the sea.

In 1956, Rachel wrote a letter to her best friend, Dorothy Freeman, about a walk she had taken while at her cabin in Maine with her grown niece, Marjorie. They had gone to the sea after a late-night storm: "To get the full wildness, we turned off our flashlights. . . . The surf was full of diamonds and emeralds. . . . A firefly was going by, his lamp blinking. . . . He was flying so low over the water . . . he was soon in trouble and we saw his light flashing urgently as he was rolled around in the wet sand. . . . You can guess the rest. . . ."

Also in 1956, Rachel wrote a piece for *Women's Home Companion* magazine called "Help Your Child to Wonder," which later became her book *The Sense of Wonder*, published in 1965. The heartfelt sentiments she shared about children and the natural world, which she described in rich detail, began with a walk on the beach with her young great-nephew and adopted son, Roger, in the early 1950s.

I combined that moment with the adventure Rachel described in her letter to Dorothy and found my own sense of wonder in that beautiful night scene of bioluminescence and the struggling firefly. All of these twinklings became my inspiration for *Night Walk to the Sea*.

My hope is that you, like Rachel and Roger, will be filled with a sense of wonder when you are outside, in nature, by the sea, in the mountains, among the forests, in your backyard, or wherever you find yourself among the creatures of the earth who depend on us for their survival.

You can read and learn much more about Rachel Carson at rachelcarson.org.

What Is Bioluminescence?

Bioluminescence is the ability of living organisms such as fireflies, deep-sea fishes, algae, jellyfish, sea stars, and even some sharks to produce their own light. The light—which is caused by a chemical reaction within these organisms—is a form of communication between members of the same species and can be produced to attract mates or prey or to ward off predators.

Often, especially after a storm, the surface of the ocean is full of bioluminescent organisms called dinoflagellates that have been stirred up from the sea floor. They are single-celled organisms that "bloom" across the water in dense layers, creating waves that sparkle at night, like the ones that Rachel and Roger see in this story.

Dinoflagellate blooms are often red. However, those that Rachel saw on her walk that night were, in her words, like "diamonds" and "emeralds," which is also indicative of a bloom of bioluminescence.

To read more about the chemical reaction that produces bioluminescence, as well as its uses, visit these pages on the Smithsonian Institution and the National Oceanic and Atmospheric Association (NOAA) websites:

ocean.si.edu/ocean-life/fish/bioluminescence

oceanexplorer.noaa.gov/facts/bioluminescence.html

To read more about a firefly's glow, visit *Scientific American:*

scientificamerican.com/article/how-and-why-do-fireflies

SELECTED READING

Books by Rachel Carson

The Edge of the Sea. Boston: Houghton Mifflin, 1955.

The Sea Around Us. New York: Oxford University Press, 1951.

The Sense of Wonder. New York: Harper and Row, 1965.

Silent Spring. Boston: Houghton Mifflin, 1962.

Under the Sea Wind: A Naturalist's Picture of Ocean Life. New York: Simon & Schuster, 1941.

Books About Rachel Carson

Brooks, Paul. *The House of Life: Rachel Carson at Work.* Boston: Houghton Mifflin, 1972.

Dunlap, Thomas R., ed. *DDT,* Silent Spring, *and the Rise of Environmentalism.* Seattle: University of Washington Press, 2008.

Erlich, Amy. *Rachel: The Story of Rachel Carson.* Illustrated by Wendell Minor. San Diego: Harcourt, Inc., 2003.

Freeman, Martha, ed. *Always, Rachel: The Letters of Rachel Carson and Dorothy Freeman, 1952–1964.* Boston: Beacon Press, 1995.

Lawlor, Laurie. *Rachel Carson and Her Book That Changed the World.* Illustrated by Laura Beingessner. New York: Holiday
      House, 2012.

Lear, Linda. *Lost Woods: The Discovered Writing of Rachel Carson.* Boston: Beacon Press, 1980.

Lear, Linda. *Rachel Carson: Witness for Nature.* New York: Henry Holt, 1997.

Levine, Ellen S. *Up Close: Rachel Carson.* New York: Viking, 2007.

ACKNOWLEDGMENTS

Heartfelt thanks to Roger Christie and Wendy Sisson, who allowed me to stay in Rachel's Southport Island cabin for a week to watch and listen and wonder and write. Thank you to Terry Young for his scientific expertise with the manuscript, to Linda Lear for her graciousness, and to naturalist friends who helped with wildlife details, as well as to the helpful folks at the Coastal Maine Botanical Gardens and the Southport General Store, who knew about freshwater ponds on Southport Island, which allowed me to have my frogs. And to Daniel Miyares—what luck that you said yes. Thank you.

To Jerry Brunner and Laurie Findlay,
and to all who wander, wonder, and care for our earth —D.W.

For Stella and Sam, my courageous explorers
and spreaders of light —D.M.

Text copyright © 2020 by Deborah Wiles   Jacket art and interior illustrations copyright © 2020 by Daniel Miyares
All rights reserved. Published in the United States by Schwartz & Wade Books, an imprint of Random House Children's Books, a division of Penguin
Random House LLC, New York.
Schwartz & Wade Books and the colophon are trademarks of Penguin Random House LLC.
Visit us on the Web! rhcbooks.com   Educators and librarians, for a variety of teaching tools, visit us at RHTeachersLibrarians.com
Library of Congress Cataloging-in-Publication Data
Names: Wiles, Deborah, author. | Miyares, Daniel, illustrator.
Title: Night walk to the sea: a story about Rachel Carson / by Deborah Wiles; illustrated by Daniel Miyares.
Description: First edition. | New York: Schwartz & Wade Books, 2020. |
Includes bibliographical references. | Audience: Ages 4–8. | Audience: Grades K–1. | Summary: One night after a storm,
environmental activist Rachel Carson takes her nephew Roger out for a walk by the sea. Includes notes about Rachel Carson,
the story, and bioluminescence.
Identifiers: LCCN 2019043194 | ISBN 978-1-5247-0147-5 (trade) | ISBN 978-1-5247-0148-2 (glb) | ISBN 978-1-5247-0149-9 (ebook)
Subjects: LCSH: Carson, Rachel, 1907–1967—Juvenile fiction. | CYAC: Carson, Rachel, 1907–1964—Fiction. | Nature—Fiction. | Seashore—Fiction. |
Night—Fiction. | Bioluminescence—Fiction.
Classification: LCC PZ7.W6474 Ni 2020 | DDC [E]—dc23
The text of this book is set in Brandon Grotesque.
The illustrations were rendered with ink on paper.

MANUFACTURED IN CHINA
2 4 6 8 10 9 7 5 3 1
First Edition